T

SIR WALTER SCOTT

Walter Scott (1770–1832) was born in Edinburgh. In his infancy he contracted a form of polio which left him lame in his right leg and led to him being sent to live for the next three years at his grandfather's farm in the Borders. Returning to Edinburgh, he was educated at the High School and Edinburgh University where, like his father before him, he studied law. He served an apprenticeship in the family practice and was called to the Bar as an advocate in 1792. In 1797 he married Charlotte Carpenter. His links with the Borders gave him an enduring interest in the history and the ballads of the region, a passion he pursued when he was appointed Sheriff-Depute for Selkirkshire in 1799, leading to the publication of his collection *The Minstrelsy of the Scottish Border* (1802–3). With an already developed interest in German literature, Scott was persuaded to try his hand at poetry of his own, leading to the long narrative poem *The Lay of the Last Minstrel* (1805) which proved a critical and financial success. This was followed by *Marmion* (1808) and, most successful of all, *The Lady of the Lake* (1810). By this time Scott had been appointed Clerk of the Court of Session in Edinburgh – a post he kept for the rest of his life – and had set up home at a little house in the Borders, which he was to develop over the years into nothing less than a baronial mansion which he called Abbotsford. The vogue for his long historical poems was passing and so he turned to prose fiction, with a manuscript he had started in 1805, subsequently published (anonymously) in 1814 as *Waverley*, a tale set during the 1745 rising. It was an immediate success and was followed by a series of historical novels produced in something of a creative explosion. These titles, later collected as The Waverley Novels ('by the author of Waverley'), included *Guy Mannering* (1815), *The Antiquary* and *Old Mortality* (1816), *Rob Roy* and *Heart of Midlothian* (1818), *The Bride of Lammermoor* and *A Legend of Montrose* (1819), *Ivanhoe*, *The Abbot* and *The Monastery* (1820), *Redgauntlet* (1824), and many more. He also wrote biographical studies and the *Tales of a Grandfather* series which retold Scottish history for the common reader.

In effect Scott's fiction invented the historical novel – with its different perspectives on past and present values – while the Scottish texts played an enormously influential part in the popular discovery of the Highlands and in the construction of a romantic vision of Scotland which has survived until practically the present day. His books were equally famous in America and in Europe readers hailed him as one of the greatest writers of his age. Scott was made a Baronet in 1818 and supervised the elaborate celebrations to mark George IV's visit to Edinburgh in 1822. When his printer and his publisher, Ballantyne and Constable, suffered a financial crash in 1826 (also the year of his wife's death), Scott's intricate investments led him into insolvency as well, and he had to redouble his writing efforts to pay off his debts – a feat finally accomplished shortly before his death. These difficult years and his poor health are movingly recorded in his *Journal*, which also reveals a fascinating picture of the times, along with his talent for friendship and the breadth of his mind. He took a sea trip to the Mediterranean in 1831, in a frigate on government service, but his health continued to fail and he returned to Abbotsford where he died in 1832.

TWO STORIES

Sir Walter Scott

2

CANONGATE POCKET CLASSICS

First published as a Pocket Classic in 2001 by
Canongate Books Ltd, 14 High Street, Edinburgh
EHI ITE.

10 9 8 7 6 5 4 3 2 I

The publishers gratefully acknowledge general sub-
sidy from the Scottish Arts Council towards the
Canongate Classics and Pocket Classics series.

Typeset in 10pt Plantin by Palimpsest Book
Production Limited, Polmont, Stirlingshire.

Printed and bound by Omnia Books, Glasgow.

CANONGATE CLASSICS
Series Editor: Roderick Watson
Editorial Board: John Pick, Cairns Craig,
Dorothy McMillan

British Library Cataloguing-in-Publication Data
A catalogue record for this volume is available
on request from the British Library.

ISBN I 84195 160 9

www.canongate.net

Wandering Willie's Tale

FROM THE DIRECTION which my guide observed, I began to suspect that the dell at Brokenburn was our probable destination; and it became important to me to consider whether I could, with propriety, or even perfect safety, intrude myself again upon the hospitality of my former host. I therefore asked Willie, whether we were bound for the Laird's, as folk called him.

'Do ye ken the Laird?' said Willie, interrupting a sonata of Corelli, of which he had whistled several bars with great precision.

'I know the Laird a little,' said I; 'and therefore I was doubting whether I ought to go to his town in disguise.'

'I should doubt not a little only, but a great deal, before I took ye there, my chap,' said Wandering Willie; 'for I am thinking it wad be worth little less than broken banes baith to you and me. Na, na, chap, we are no ganging to the Laird's, but to a blithe birling at the Brokenburn-foot, where there will be mony a braw lad and lass; and maybe there may be some of the Laird's folks, for he never comes to sic splores himsell. He is all for fowling-piece and salmon-spear, now that pike and musket are out of the question.'

'He has been a soldier, then?' said I.

'I'se warrant him a soger,' answered Willie; 'but take my advice, and speer as little about him as he does about you. Best to let sleeping dogs lie. Better say naething about the Laird, my man, and tell me instead, what sort of a chap ye are, that are sae ready to cleik in with an auld gaberlunzie fiddler? Maggie says ye're gentle, but a shilling maks a' the difference that Maggie kens, between a gentle and a semple, and your crowns wad mak ye a prince of the blood in her een. But I am ane that ken full weel that ye may wear good claithes, and have a saft hand, and yet that may come of idleness as weel as gentrice.'

I told him my name, with the same addition I had formerly given to Mr Joshua Geddes; that I was a law-student, tired of my studies, and rambling about for exercise and amusement.

'And are ye in the wont of drawing up wi' a' the gangrel bodies that ye meet on the high-road, or find cowering in a sand-bunker upon the links?' demanded Willie.

'Oh no, only with honest folks like yourself, Willie,' was my reply.

'Honest folks like me! – How do ye ken whether

I am honest, or what I am? – I may be the deevil himsell for what ye ken; for he has power to come disguised like an angel of light; and besides, he is a prime fiddler. He played a sonata to Corelli, ye ken.'

There was something odd in this speech, and the tone in which it was said. It seemed as if my companion was not always in his constant mind, or that he was willing to try if he could frighten me. I laughed at the extravagance of his language, however, and asked him in reply, if he was fool enough to believe that the foul fiend would play so silly a masquerade.

'Ye ken little about it – little about it,' said the old man, shaking his head and beard, and knitting his brows – 'I could tell ye something about that.'

What his wife mentioned of his being a tale-teller, as well as a musician, now occurred to me; and as you know I like tales of superstition, I begged to have a specimen of his talent as we went along.

'It is very true,' said the blind man, 'that when I am tired of scraping thairm or singing ballants, I whiles mak a tale serve the turn among the country bodies; and I have some fearsome anes, that make the auld carlines shake on the settle, and the bits o' bairns skirl on their minnies out frae their beds. But this that I am gaun to tell you was a thing that befell in our ain house in my father's time – that is, my father was then a hafflins callant; and I tell it to you, that it may be a lesson to you, that are but a young, thoughtless chap, wha ye draw up wi' on a lonely road; for muckle was the dool and care that came o't to my gudesire.'

He commenced his tale accordingly, in a distinct narrative tone of voice, which he raised and depressed with considerable skill; at times sinking almost into a whisper, and turning his clear but sightless eyeballs upon my face, as if it had been possible for him to witness the impression which his narrative made upon my features. I will not spare you a syllable of it, although it be of the longest; so I make a dash —— and begin.

WANDERING WILLIE'S TALE

YE MAUN HAVE heard of Sir Robert Redgauntlet of that Ilk, who lived in these parts before the dear years. The country will lang mind him; and our fathers used to draw breath thick if ever they heard him named. He was out wi' the Hielandmen in Montrose's time; and again he was in the hills

wi' Glencairn in the saxteen hundred and fifty-
twa; and sae when King Charles the Second
came in, wha was in sic favour as the Laird of
Redgauntlet? He was knighted at Lonon court,
wi' the King's ain sword; and being a red-hot
prelatist, he came down here, rampauging like
a lion, with commissions of lieutenancy (and of
lunacy, for what I ken), to put down a' the Whigs
and Covenanters in the country. Wild wark they
made of it; for the Whigs were as dour as the
Cavaliers were fierce, and it was which should
first tire the other. Redgauntlet was aye for the
strong hand; and his name is kend as wide in
the country as Claverhouse's or Tam Dalyell's.
Glen, nor dargle, nor mountain, nor cave, could
hide the puir hill-folk when Redgauntlet was out
with bugle and bloodhound after them, as if they
had been sae mony deer. And troth when they fand
them, they didna mak muckle mair ceremony than
a Hielandman wi' a roebuck – It was just, 'Will ye
tak the test?' – if not, 'Make ready – present – fire!'
and there lay the recusant.

Far and wide was Sir Robert hated and feared.
Men thought he had a direct compact with Satan
– that he was proof against steel – and that bullets
happed aff his buff-coat like hailstanes from a hearth
– that he had a mear that would turn a hare on the

side of Carrifra-gawns[1] – and muckle to the same purpose, of whilk mair anon. The best blessing they wared on him was, 'Deil scowp wi' Redgauntlet!' He wasna a bad master to his ain folk, though, and was weel aneugh liked by his tenants; and as for the lackies and troopers that raid out wi' him to the persecutions, as the Whigs caa'd those killing times, they wad hae drunken themsells blind to his health at ony time.

Now you are to ken that my gudesire lived on Redgauntlet's grund – they ca' the place Primrose-Knowe. We had lived on the grund, and under the Redgauntlets, since the riding-days, and lang before. It was a pleasant bit; and I think the air is callerer and fresher there than ony where else in the country. It's a' deserted now; and I sat on the broken door-cheek three days since, and was glad I couldna see the plight the place was in; but that's a' wide o' the mark. There dwelt my gudesire, Steenie Steenson, a rambling, rattling chiel' he had been in his young days, and could play weel on the pipes; he was famous at 'Hoopers and Girders' – a' Cumberland couldna touch him at 'Jockie Lattin' – and he had the finest finger for the back-lilt between Berwick and Carlisle. The like o' Steenie wasna the

---

[1] A precipitous side of a mountain in Moffatdale.

sort that they made Whigs o'. And so he became a Tory, as they ca' it, which we now ca' Jacobites, just out of a kind of needcessity, that he might belang to some side or other. He had nae ill-will to the Whig bodies, and liked little to see the blude rin, though, being obliged to follow Sir Robert in hunting and hoisting, watching and warding, he saw muckle mischief, and maybe did some, that he couldna avoid.

Now Steenie was a kind of favourite with his master, and kend a' the folks about the castle, and was often sent for to play the pipes when they were at their merriment. Auld Dougal MacCallum, the butler, that had followed Sir Robert through gude and ill, thick and thin, pool and stream, was specially fond of the pipes, and aye gae my gudesire his gude word wi' the Laird; for Dougal could turn his master round his finger.

Weel, round came the Revolution, and it had like to have broken the hearts baith of Dougal and his master. But the change was not a'thegether sae great as they feared, and other folk thought for. The Whigs made an unco crawing what they wad do with their auld enemies, and in special wi' Sir Robert Redgauntlet. But there were ower mony great folks dipped in the same doings, to mak a spick and span new warld. So Parliament passed it a' ower easy; and

Sir Robert, bating that he was held to hunting foxes instead of Covenanters, remained just the man he was. His revel was as loud, and his hall as weel lighted, as ever it had been, though maybe he lacked the fines of the nonconformists, that used to come to stock his larder and cellar; for it is certain he began to be keener about the rents than his tenants used to find him before, and they behoved to be prompt to the rent-day, or else the Laird wasna pleased. And he was sic an awsome body, that naebody cared to anger him; for the oaths he swore, and the rage that he used to get into, and the looks that he put on, made men sometimes think him a devil incarnate.

Weel, my gudesire was nae manager – no that he was a very great misguider – but he hadna the saving gift, and he got twa terms' rent in arrear. He got the first brash at Whitsunday put ower wi' fair word and piping; but when Martinmas came, there was a summons from the grund-officer to come wi' the rent on a day preceese, or else Steenie behoved to flit. Sair wark he had to get the siller; but he was weel-freended, and at last he got the haill scraped thegether – a thousand merks – the maist of it was from a neighbour they caa'd Laurie Lapraik – a sly tod. Laurie had walth o' gear – could hunt wi' the hound and rin wi' the hare – and be Whig or Tory, saunt or sinner, as the wind stood. He was a professor in this Revolution warld, but he liked an orra sough of this warld, and a tune on the pipes weel aneugh at a bytime; and abune a', he thought he had gude security for the siller he lent my gudesire ower the stocking at Primrose Knowe.

Away trots my gudesire to Redgauntlet Castle wi' a heavy purse and a light heart, glad to be out of the Laird's danger. Weel, the first thing he learned at the Castle was, that Sir Robert had fretted himsell into a fit of the gout, because he did not appear before twelve o'clock. It wasna a'thegether for sake of the money, Dougal thought; but because he didna like to part wi' my gudesire aff the grund. Dougal was glad to see Steenie, and brought him into the great oak parlour, and there sat the Laird his leesome lane, excepting that he had beside him a great, ill-favoured jackanape, that was a special pet of his; a cankered beast it was, and mony an ill-natured trick it played – ill to please it was, and easily angered – ran about the haill castle, chattering and yowling, and pinching, and biting folk, specially before ill-weather, or disturbances in the state. Sir Robert caa'd it Major Weir, after the warlock that was burnt;[2] and few folk liked either the name or the conditions of the creature – they thought there

---

[2] A celebrated wizard, executed at Edinburgh for sorcery and other crimes.

was something in it by ordinar – and my gudesire
was not just easy in mind when the door shut on
him, and he saw himself in the room wi' naebody
but the Laird, Dougal MacCallum, and the Major,
a thing that hadna chanced to him before.

Sir Robert sat, or, I should say, lay, in a great
armed chair, wi' his grand velvet gown, and his feet
on a cradle; for he had baith gout and gravel, and
his face looked as gash and ghastly as Satan's. Major
Weir sat opposite to him, in a red laced coat, and
the Laird's wig on his head; and aye as Sir Robert
girned wi' pain, the jackanape girned too, like a
sheep's head between a pair of tangs – an ill-faur'd,
fearsome couple they were. The Laird's buff-coat
was hung on a pin behind him, and his broadsword
and his pistols within reach; for he keepit up the auld
fashion of having the weapons ready, and a horse
saddled day and night, just as he used to do when
he was able to loup on horseback, and away after
ony of the hill-folk he could get speerings of. Some
said it was for fear of the Whigs taking vengeance,
but I judge it was just his auld custom – he wasna
gien to fear onything. The rental-book, wi' its black
cover and brass clasps, was lying beside him; and a
book of sculduddry sangs was put betwixt the leaves,
to keep it open at the place where it bore evidence
against the Goodman of Primrose Knowe, as behind

the hand with his mails and duties. Sir Robert gave my gudesire a look, as if he would have withered his heart in his bosom. Ye maun ken he had a way of bending his brows, that men saw the visible mark of a horseshoe in his forehead, deep dinted, as if it had been stamped there.

'Are ye come light-handed, ye son of a toom whistle?' said Sir Robert. 'Zounds! if you are—'

My gudesire, with as gude a countenance as he could put on, made a leg, and placed the bag of money on the table wi' a dash, like a man that does something clever. The Laird drew it to him hastily – 'Is it all here, Steenie, man?'

'Your honour will find it right,' said my gudesire.

'Here, Dougal,' said the Laird, 'gie Steenie a tass of brandy downstairs, till I count the siller and write the receipt.'

But they werena weel out of the room, when Sir Robert gied a yelloch that garr'd the Castle rock. Back ran Dougal – in flew the livery-men – yell on yell gied the Laird, ilk ane mair awfu' than the ither. My gudesire knew not whether to stand or flee, but he ventured back into the parlour, where a' was gaun hirdy-girdie – naebody to say 'come in,' or 'gae out.' Terribly the Laird roared for cauld water to his feet, and wine to cool his throat; and Hell, hell, hell, and its flames, was aye

the word in his mouth. They brought him water,
and when they plunged his swoln feet into the tub,
he cried out it was burning; and folk say that it *did*
bubble and sparkle like a seething caldron. He flung
the cup at Dougal's head, and said he had given
him blood instead of burgundy; and, sure aneugh,
the lass washed clotted blood aff the carpet the
neist day. The jackanape they caa'd Major Weir,
it jibbered and cried as if it was mocking its master;
my gudesire's head was like to turn – he forgot baith
siller and receipt, and downstairs he banged; but as
he ran, the shrieks came faint and fainter; there was a
deep-drawn shivering groan, and word gaed through
the Castle that the Laird was dead.

Weel, away came my gudesire, wi' his finger in
his mouth, and his best hope was, that Dougal had
seen the money-bag, and heard the Laird speak
of writing the receipt. The young Laird, now Sir
John, came from Edinburgh, to see things put to
rights. Sir John and his father never gree'd weel.
Sir John had been bred an advocate, and after-
wards sat in the last Scots Parliament and voted
for the Union, having gotten, it was thought, a
rug of the compensations – if his father could have
come out of his grave, he would have brained him
for it on his awn hearthstane. Some thought it
was easier counting with the auld rough Knight

than the fair-spoken young ane – but mair of that anon.

Dougal MacCallum, poor body, neither grat nor grained, but gaed about the house looking like a corpse, but directing, as was his duty, a' the order of the grand funeral. Now, Dougal looked aye waur and waur when night was coming, and was aye the last to gang to his bed, whilk was in a little round just opposite the chamber of dais, whilk his master occupied while he was living, and where he now lay in state, as they caa'd it, weel-a-day! The night before the funeral, Dougal could keep his awn counsel nae langer; he came doun with his proud spirit, and fairly asked auld Hutcheon to sit in his room with him for an hour. When they were in the round, Dougal took ae tass of brandy to himsell, and gave another to Hutcheon, and wished him all health and lang life, and said that, for himsell, he wasna lang for this world; for that, every night since Sir Robert's death, his silver call had sounded from the state chamber, just as it used to do at nights in his lifetime, to call Dougal to help to turn him in his bed. Dougal said, that being alone with the dead on that floor of the tower (for naebody cared to wake Sir Robert Redgauntlet like another corpse), he had never daured to answer the call, but that now his conscience checked him for neglecting his duty; for, 'though death breaks service,' said MacCallum, 'it shall never break my service to Sir Robert; and I will answer his next whistle, so be you will stand by me, Hutcheon.'

Hutcheon had nae will to the wark, but he had stood by Dougal in battle and broil, and he wad not fail him at this pinch; so down the carles sat ower a stoup of brandy, and Hutcheon, who was something of a clerk, would have read a chapter of the Bible; but Dougal would hear naething but a blaud of Davie Lindsay, whilk was the waur preparation.

When midnight came, and the house was quiet as the grave, sure enough the silver whistle sounded as sharp and shrill as if Sir Robert was blowing it, and up got the twa auld serving-men, and tottered into the room where the dead man lay. Hutcheon saw aneugh at the first glance; for there were torches in the room, which showed him the foul fiend, in his ain shape, sitting on the Laird's coffin! Ower he cowped as if he had been dead. He could not tell how lang he lay in a trance at the door, but when he gathered himself, he cried on his neighbour, and getting nae answer, raised the house, when Dougal was found lying dead within twa steps of the bed where his master's coffin was placed. As for the whistle, it was gane anes and aye; but mony a time was it heard at the top of the house on the bartizan, and amang the auld chimneys and turrets where the howlets have their nests. Sir John hushed the matter up, and the funeral passed over without mair bogle-wark.

But when a' was ower, and the Laird was beginning to settle his affairs, every tenant was called up for his arrears, and my gudesire for the full sum that stood against him in the rental-book. Weel, away he trots to the Castle, to tell his story, and there he is introduced to Sir John, sitting in his father's chair, in deep mourning, with weepers and hanging cravat, and a small walking rapier by his side, instead of the auld broadsword that had a hundred-weight of steel about it, what with blade, chape, and basket-hilt. I have heard their communing so often tauld ower, that I almost think I was there mysell, though I couldna be born at the time. (In fact, Alan, my companion mimicked, with a good deal of humour, the flattering, conciliating tone of the tenant's address, and the hypocritical melancholy of the Laird's reply. His grandfather, he said, had, while he spoke, his eye fixed on the rental-book, as if it were a mastiff-dog that he was afraid would spring up and bite him.)

'I wuss ye joy, sir, of the head seat, and the white loaf, and the braid lairdship. Your father was a kind man to friends and followers; muckle grace to you,

Sir John, to fill his shoon – his boots, I suld say, for he seldom wore shoon, unless it were muils when he had the gout.'

'Ay, Steenie,' quoth the Laird, sighing deeply, and putting his napkin to his een, 'his was a sudden call, and he will be missed in the country; no time to set his house in order – weel prepared Godward, no doubt, which is the root of the matter – but left us behind a tangled hesp to wind, Steenie. – Hem! hem! We maun go to business, Steenie; much to do, and little time to do it in.'

Here he opened the fatal volume. I have heard of a thing they call Doomsday-book – I am clear it has been a rental of back-ganging tenants.

'Stephen,' said Sir John, still in the same soft, sleekit tone of voice – 'Stephen Stevenson or Steenson, ye are down here for a year's rent behind the hand – due at last term.'

Stephen. – 'Please your honour, Sir John, I paid it to your father.'

Sir John. – 'Ye took a receipt, then, doubtless, Stephen; and can produce it?'

Stephen. – 'Indeed, I hadna time, an it like your honour; for nae sooner had I set doun the siller, and just as his honour, Sir Robert, that's gaen, drew it till him to count it, and write out the receipt, he was ta'en wi' the pains that removed him.'

'That was unlucky,' said Sir John, after a pause. 'But ye maybe paid it in the presence of somebody. I want but a *talis qualis* evidence, Stephen. I would *go ower* strictly to work with no poor man.'

Stephen. – 'Troth, Sir John, there was naebody in the room but Dougal MacCallum the butler. But, as your honour kens, he has e'en followed his auld master.'

'Very unlucky again, Stephen,' said Sir John, without altering his voice a single note. 'The man to whom ye paid the money is dead – and the man who witnessed the payment is dead too – and the siller, which should have been to the fore, is neither seen nor heard tell of in the repositories. How am I to believe a' this?'

Stephen. – 'I dinna ken, your honour; but there is a bit memorandum note of the very coins; for, God help me! I had to borrow out of twenty purses; and I am sure that ilka man there set down will take his grit oath for what purpose I borrowed the money.'

Sir John. – 'I have little doubt ye *borrowed* the money, Steenie. It is the *payment* to my father that I want to have some proof of.'

Stephen. – 'The siller maun be about the house, Sir John. And since your honour never got it, and his honour that was canna have taen it wi' him, maybe some of the family may have seen it.'

Sir John. – 'We will examine the servants, Stephen; that is but reasonable.'

But lackey and lass, and page and groom, all denied stoutly that they had ever seen such a bag of money as my gudesire described. What was waur, he had unluckily not mentioned to any living soul of them his purpose of paying his rent. Ae quean had noticed something under his arm, but she took it for the pipes.

Sir John Redgauntlet ordered the servants out of the room, and then said to my gudesire, 'Now, Steenie, ye see ye have fair play; and, as I have little doubt ye ken better where to find the siller than ony other body, I beg, in fair terms, and for your own sake, that you will end this fasherie; for, Stephen, ye maun pay or flit.'

'The Lord forgie your opinion,' said Stephen, driven almost to his wit's end – 'I am an honest man.'

'So am I, Stephen,' said his honour; 'and so are all the folks in the house, I hope. But if there be a knave amongst us, it must be he that tells the story he cannot prove.' He paused, and then added, mair sternly, 'If I understand your trick, sir, you want to take advantage of some malicious reports concerning things in this family, and particularly respecting my father's sudden death, thereby to cheat me out of the money, and perhaps take away my character, by insinuating that I have received the rent I am demanding. – Where do you suppose this money to be? – I insist upon knowing.'

My gudesire saw everything look so muckle against him, that he grew nearly desperate – however he shifted from one foot to another, looked to every corner of the room, and made no answer.

'Speak out, sirrah,' said the Laird, assuming a look of his father's, a very particular ane, which he had when he was angry; it seemed as if the wrinkles of his frown made that self-same fearful shape of a horse's shoe in the middle of his brow; – 'Speak out, sir! I *will* know your thoughts; – do you suppose that I have this money?'

'Far be it frae me to say so,' said Stephen.

'Do you charge any of my people with having taken it?'

'I wad be laith to charge them that may be innocent,' said my gudesire; 'and if there be any one that is guilty, I have nae proof.'

'Somewhere the money must be, if there is a word of truth in your story,' said Sir John; 'I ask where you think it is – and demand a correct answer?'

'In hell if you *will* have my thoughts of it,' said my gudesire, driven to extremity, – 'In hell! with your father, his jackanape, and his silver whistle.'

Down the stairs he ran (for the parlour was nae place for him after such a word), and he heard the Laird swearing blood and wounds, behind him, as fast as ever did Sir Robert, and roaring for the bailie and the baron-officer.

Away rode my gudesire to his chief creditor (him they caa'd Laurie Lapraik), to try if he could make onything out of him; but when he tauld his story, he got but the worst word in his wame – thief, beggar, and dyvour, were the saftest terms; and to the boot of these hard terms, Laurie brought up the auld story of his dipping his hand in the blood of God's saunts, just as if a tenant could have helped riding with the Laird, and that a laird like Sir Robert Redgauntlet. My gudesire was, by this time, far beyond the bounds of patience, and, while he and Laurie were at deil speed the liars, he was wanchancie aneugh to abuse Lapraik's doctrine as weel as the man, and said things that garr'd folks' flesh grue that heard them; – he wasna just himsell, and he had lived wi' a wild set in his day.

At last they parted, and my gudesire was to ride hame through the wood of Pitmurkie, that is a' fou of black firs, as they say. – I ken the wood, but the firs may be black or white for what I can tell. – At the entry of the wood there is a wild common, and on the edge of the common, a little lonely change-house, that was keepit then by an ostler wife, they suld hae caa'd her Tibbie Faw, and there puir Steenie cried for a mutchkin of brandy, for he had had no refreshment the haill day. Tibbie was earnest wi' him to take a bite of meat, but he couldna think o't, nor would he take his foot out of the stirrup, and took off the brandy wholely at twa draughts, and named a toast at each: – the first was, the memory of Sir Robert Redgauntlet, and might he never lie quiet in his grave till he had righted his poor bond-tenant; and the second was, a health to Man's Enemy, if he would but get him back the pock of siller, or tell him what came o't, for he saw the haill world was like to regard him as a thief and a cheat, and he took that waur than even the ruin of his house and hauld.

On he rode, little caring where. It was a dark night turned, and the trees made it yet darker, and he let the beast take its ain road through the wood; when all of a sudden, from tired and wearied that it was before, the nag began to spring, and flee, and stend, that my gudesire could hardly keep the saddle – Upon the whilk, a horseman, suddenly riding up beside him, said, 'That's a mettle beast of yours, freend; will you sell him?' – So saying, he touched the horse's neck with his riding-wand, and it fell into its auld heigh-ho of a stumbling trot. 'But his spunk's soon out of him, I think,' continued the stranger, 'and that is like mony a man's courage, that thinks he wad do great things till he come to the proof.'

My gudesire scarce listened to this, but spurred his horse, with 'Gude e'en to you, freend.'

But it's like the stranger was ane that doesna lightly yield his point; for, ride as Steenie liked, he was aye beside him at the self-same pace. At last my gudesire, Steenie Steenson, grew half angry; and, to say the truth, half feared.

'What is it that ye want with me, freend?' he said. 'If ye be a robber, I have nae money; if ye be a leal man, wanting company, I have nae heart to mirth or speaking; and if ye want to ken the road, I scarce ken it mysell.'

'If you will tell me your grief,' said the stranger, I am one, that, though I have been sair miscaa'd in the world, am the only hand for helping my freends.'

So my gudesire, to ease his ain heart, mair than from any hope of help, told him the story from beginning to end.

'It's a hard pinch,' said the stranger; 'but I think I can help you.'

'If you could lend the money, sir, and take a lang day – I ken nae other help on earth,' said my gudesire.

'But there may be some under the earth,' said the stranger. 'Come, I'll be frank wi' you; I could lend you the money on bond, but you would maybe scruple my terms. Now, I can tell you, that your auld Laird is disturbed in his grave by your curses, and the wailing of your family, and if ye daur venture to go to see him, he will give you the receipt.'

My gudesire's hair stood on end at this proposal, but he thought his companion might be some humorsome chield that was trying to frighten him, and might end with lending him the money. Besides, he was bauld wi' brandy, and desperate wi' distress; and he said he had courage to go to the gate of hell, and a step farther, for that receipt. – The stranger laughed.

Weel, they rode on through the thickest of the wood, when, all of a sudden, the horse stopped at the door of a great house; and, but that he knew the place was ten miles off, my father would have thought he was at Redgauntlet Castle. They rode into the outer courtyard, through the muckle faulding yetts, and aneath the auld portcullis; and the whole front of the house was lighted, and there were pipes and fiddles, and as much dancing and deray within as used to be at Sir Robert's house at Pace and Yule, and such high seasons. They lap off, and my gudesire, as seemed to him, fastened his horse to the very ring he had tied him to that morning, when he gaed to wait on the young Sir John.

'God!' said my gudesire, 'if Sir Robert's death be but a dream!'

He knocked at the ha' door just as he was wont, and his auld acquaintance, Dougal MacCallum, – just after his wont, too, – came to open the door, and said, 'Piper Steenie, are ye there, lad? Sir Robert has been crying for you.'

My gudesire was like a man in a dream – he looked for the stranger, but he was gane for the time. At last he just tried to say, 'Ha! Dougal Driveower, are ye living? I thought ye had been dead.'

'Never fash yoursell wi' me,' said Dougal, 'but look to yoursell; and see ye tak naething frae onybody here, neither meat, drink, or siller, except just the receipt that is your ain.'

So saying, he led the way out through halls and trances that were weel kend to my gudesire, and into the auld oak parlour; and there was as much singing of profane sangs, and birling of red wine, and speaking blasphemy and sculduddry, as had ever been in Redgauntlet Castle when it was at the blithest.

But, Lord take us in keeping, what a set of ghastly revellers they were that sat around that table! – My gudesire kend mony that had long before gane to their place, for often had he piped to the most part in the hall of Redgauntlet. There was the fierce Middleton, and the dissolute Rothes, and the crafty Lauderdale; and Dalyell, with his bauld head and a beard to his girdle; and Earlshall, with Cameron's blude on his hand; and wild Bonshaw, that tied blessed Mr Cargill's limbs till the blude sprung; and Dunbarton Douglas, the twice-turned traitor baith to country and king. There was the Bluidy Advocate MacKenyle, who, for his worldly wit and wisdom had been to the rest as a god. And there was Claverhouse, as beautiful as when he lived, with his long, dark, curled locks, streaming down over his laced buff-coat, and his left hand always on his right spule-blade, to hide the wound that the silver bullet had made. He sat apart from them all, and looked at them with a melancholy, haughty countenance; while the rest hallooed, and sung, and laughed, that the room rang. But their smiles were fearfully contorted from time to time; and their laugh passed into such wild sounds, as made my gudesire's very nails grow blue, and chilled the marrow in his banes.

They that waited at the table were just the wicked serving-men and troopers, that had done their work and cruel bidding on earth. There was the Lang Lad of the Nethertown, that helped to take Argyle; and the Bishop's summoner, that they called the Deil's Rattle-bag; and the wicked guardsmen in their laced coats; and the savage Highland Amorites, that shed blood like water; and many a proud serving-man, haughty of heart and bloody of hand, cringing to the rich, and making them wickeder than they would be; grinding the poor to powder, when the rich had broken them to fragments. And mony, mony mair were coming and ganging, a' as busy in their vocation as if they had been alive.

Sir Robert Redgauntlet, in the midst of a' this fearful riot, cried, wi' a voice like thunder, on Steenie Piper to come to the board-head where he was sitting; his legs stretched out before him, and swathed up with flannel, with his holster pistols aside him, while the great broadsword rested against his chair, just as my gudesire had seen him the last time upon earth – the very cushion for the jackanape was close to him, but the creature itsell was not there – it wasna its hour, it's likely; for he heard them say, as he came forward, 'Is not the Major come yet?' And another answered, 'The jackanape will be here betimes the morn.' And when my gudesire came forward, Sir Robert, or his ghaist, or the deevil in his likeness, said, 'Weel, piper, hae ye settled wi' my son for the year's rent?'

With much ado my father gat breath to say,

that Sir John would not settle without his honour's receipt.

'Ye shall hae that for a tune of the pipes, Steenie,' said the appearance of Sir Robert – 'Play us up "Weel hoddled, Luckie."'

Now this was a tune my gudesire learned frae a warlock, that heard it when they were worshipping Satan at their meetings; and my gudesire had sometimes played it at the ranting suppers in Redgauntlet Castle, but never very willingly; and now he grew cauld at the very name of it, and said, for excuse, he hadna his pipes wi' him.

'MacCallum, ye limb of Beelzebub,' said the fearfu' Sir Robert, 'bring Steenie the pipes that I am keeping for him!'

MacCallum brought a pair of pipes might have served the piper of Donald of the Isles. But he gave my gudesire a nudge as he offered them; and looking secretly and closely, Steenie saw that the chanter was of steel, and heated to a white heat; so he had fair warning not to trust his fingers with it. So he excused himself again, and said, he was faint and frightened, and had not wind aneugh to fill the bag.

'Then ye maun eat and drink, Steenie,' said the figure; 'for we do little else here; and it's ill speaking between a fou man and a fasting.'

Now these were the very words that the bloody

Earl of Douglas said to keep the King's messenger
in hand, while he cut the head off MacLellan of
Bombie, at the Threave Castle, and that put Steenie
mair and mair on his guard. So he spoke up like a
man, and said he came neither to eat, or drink, or
make minstrelsy; but simply for his ain – to ken what
was come o' the money he had paid, and to get a
discharge for it; and he was so stout-hearted by this
time, that he charged Sir Robert for conscience-sake
– (he had no power to say the holy name) – and as
he hoped for peace and rest, to spread no snares for
him, but just to give him his ain.

The appearance gnashed its teeth and laughed,
but it took from a large pocket-book the receipt,
and handed it to Steenie. 'There is your receipt, ye
pitiful cur; and for the money, my dog-whelp of a
son may go look for it in the Cat's Cradle.'

My gudesire uttered mony thanks, and was about
to retire, when Sir Robert roared aloud, 'Stop,
though, thou sack-doubling son of a whore! I am not
done with thee. HERE we do nothing for nothing;
and you must return on this very day twelvemonth,
to pay your master the homage that you owe me for
my protection.'

My father's tongue was loosed of a suddenty, and
he said aloud, 'I refer mysell to God's pleasure, and
not to yours.'

He had no sooner uttered the word than all was dark around him; and he sunk on the earth with such a sudden shock, that he lost both breath and sense.

How lang Steenie lay there, he could not tell; but when he came to himsell, he was lying in the auld kirkyard of Redgauntlet parochine, just at the door of the family aisle, and the skutcheon of the auld knight, Sir Robert, hanging over his head. There was a deep morning fog on grass and gravestane around him, and his horse was feeding quietly beside the minister's twa cows. Steenie would have thought the whole was a dream, but he had the receipt in his hand, fairly written and signed by the auld Laird; only the last letters of his name were a little disorderly, written like one seized with sudden pain.

Sorely troubled in his mind, he left that dreary place, rode through the mist to Redgauntlet Castle, and with much ado he got speech of the Laird.

'Well, you dyvour bankrupt,' was the first word, 'have you brought me my rent?'

'No,' answered my gudesire, 'I have not; but I have brought your honour Sir Robert's receipt for it.'

'How, sirrah? – Sir Robert's receipt! – You told me he had not given you one.'

'Will your honour please to see if that bit line is right?'

Sir John looked at every line, and at every letter, with much attention; and at last at the date, which my gudesire had not observed, – '*From my appointed place,*' he read, '*this twenty-fifth of November.*' – 'What! – That is yesterday! – Villain, thou must have gone to hell for this!'

'I got it from your honour's father – whether he be in heaven or hell, I know not,' said Steenie.

'I will delate you for a warlock to the Privy Council!' said Sir John. 'I will send you to your master, the devil, with the help of a tar-barrel and a torch!'

'I intend to delate mysell to the Presbytery,' said Steenie, 'and tell them all I have seen last night, whilk are things fitter for them to judge of than a borrel man like me.'

Sir John paused, composed himself, and desired to hear the full history; and my gudesire told it him from point to point, as I have told it you – word for word, neither more nor less.

Sir John was silent again for a long time, and at last he said, very composedly, 'Steenie, this story of yours concerns the honour of many a noble family besides mine; and if it be a leasing-making, to keep yourself out of my danger, the least you can expect is to have a redhot iron driven through your tongue, and that will be as bad as scauding your fingers wi' a redhot chanter. But yet it may be true, Steenie; and if the money cast up, I shall not know what to think of it. – But where shall we find the Cat's Cradle? There are cats enough about the old house, but I think they kitten without the ceremony of bed or cradle.'

'We were best ask Hutcheon,' said my gudesire; 'he kens a' the odd corners about as weel as – another serving-man that is now gane, and that I wad not like to name.'

Aweel, Hutcheon, when he was asked, told them, that a ruinous turret, lang disused, next to the clock-house, only accessible by a ladder, for the opening was on the outside, and far above the battlements, was called of old the Cat's Cradle.

'There will I go immediately,' said Sir John; and he took (with what purpose, Heaven kens) one of his father's pistols from the hall-table, where they had lain since the night he died, and hastened to the battlements.

It was a dangerous place to climb, for the ladder was auld and frail, and wanted ane or twa rounds. However, up got Sir John, and entered at the turret door, where his body stopped the only little light that was in the bit turret. Something flees at him

wi' a vengeance, maist dang him back ower – bang
gaed the knight's pistol, and Hutcheon, that held
the ladder, and my gudesire that stood beside him,
hears a loud skelloch. A minute after, Sir John flings
the body of the jackanape down to them, and cries
that the siller is fund, and that they should come
up and help him. And there was the bag of siller
sure eneugh, and mony orra thing besides, that had
been missing for mony a day. And Sir John, when
he had riped the turret weel, led my gudesire into
the dining-parlour, and took him by the hand, and
spoke kindly to him, and said he was sorry he should
have doubted his word, and that he would hereafter
be a good master to him, to make amends.

'And now, Steenie,' said Sir John, 'although this
vision of yours tend, on the whole, to my father's
credit, as an honest man, that he should, even after
his death, desire to see justice done to a poor man
like you, yet you are sensible that ill-dispositioned
men might make bad constructions upon it, concerning his soul's health. So, I think, we had better
lay the haill dirdum on that ill-deedie creature,
Major Weir, and say naething about your dream
in the wood of Pitmurkie. You had taken ower
muckle brandy to be very certain about onything;
and, Steenie, this receipt' (his hand shook while he
held it out), – 'it's but a queer kind of document,

and we will do best, I think, to put it quietly in the fire.'

'Od, but for as queer as it is, it's a' the voucher I have for my rent,' said my gudesire, who was afraid, it may be, of losing the benefit of Sir Robert's discharge.

'I will bear the contents to your credit in the rental-book, and give you a discharge under my own hand,' said Sir John, 'and that on the spot. And, Steenie, if you can hold your tongue about this matter, you shall sit, from this term downward, at an easier rent.'

'Mony thanks to your honour,' said Steenie, who saw easily in what corner the wind was; 'doubtless I will be conformable to all your honour's commands; only I would willingly speak wi' some powerful minister on the subject, for I do not like the sort of soumans of appointment whilk your honour's father—'

'Do not call the phantom my father!' said Sir John, interrupting him.

'Weel, then, the thing that was so like him,' said my gudesire; 'he spoke of my coming back to see him this time twelve-month, and it's a weight on my conscience.'

'Aweel, then,' said Sir John, 'if you be so much distressed in mind, you may speak to our minister of

the parish; he is a douce man, regards the honour of
our family, and the mair that he may look for some
patronage from me.'

Wi' that, my father readily agreed that the receipt
should be burnt, and the Laird threw it into the
chimney with his ain hand. Burn it would not for
them, though; but away it flew up the lum, wi' a
lang train of sparks at its tail, and a hissing noise
like a squib.

My grandsire gaed down to the Manse, and the
minister, when he had heard the story, said, it was
his real opinion, that though my gudesire had gaen
very far in tempering with dangerous matters, yet,
as he had refused the devil's arles (for such was the
offer of meat and drink), and had refused to do
homage by piping at his bidding, he hoped, that if
he held a circumspect walk hereafter, Satan could
take little advantage by what was come and gane.
And, indeed, my gudesire, of his ain accord, lang
forswore baith the pipes and the brandy – it was
not even till the year was out, and the fatal day
past, that he would so much as take the fiddle, or
drink usquebaugh or tippeny.

Sir John made up his story about the jackanape as
he liked himself; and some believe till this day there
was no more in the matter than the filching nature
of the brute. Indeed, ye'll no hinder some to threap,

that it was nane o' the auld Enemy that Dougal and my gudesire saw in the Laird's room, but only that wanchancy creature, the Major, capering on the coffin; and that, as to the blawing on the Laird's whistle that was heard after he was dead, the filthy brute could do that as weel as the Laird himsell, if no better. But Heaven kens the truth, whilk first came out by the minister's wife, after Sir John and her ain gudeman were baith in the moulds. And then my gudesire, wha was failed in his limbs, but not in his judgment or memory – at least nothing to speak of – was obliged to tell the real narrative to his friends, for the credit of his good name. He might else have been charged for a warlock.

The shades of evening were growing thicker around us as my conductor finished his long narrative with this moral – 'Ye see, birkie, it is nae chancy thing to tak a stranger traveller for a guide, when you are in an uncouth land.'

'I should not have made that inference,' said I. 'Your grandfather's adventure was fortunate for himself, whom it saved from ruin and distress; and fortunate for his landlord also, whom it prevented from committing a gross act of injustice.'

'Ay, but they had baith to sup the sauce o't sooner or later,' said Wandering Willie – 'what was fristed wasna forgiven. Sir John died before he was much over threescore; and it was just like of a moment's illness. And for my gudesire, though he departed in fulness of life, yet there was my father, a yauld man of forty-five, fell down betwixt the stilts of his pleugh, and raise never again, and left nae bairn but me, a puir sightless, fatherless, motherless creature, could neither work nor want. Things gaed weel eneugh at first; for Sir Redwald Redgauntlet, the only son of Sir John, and the oye of auld Sir Robert, and, waes me! the last of the honourable house, took the farm aff our hands, and brought me into his household to have care of me. He liked music, and I had the best teachers baith England and Scotland could gie me. Mony a merry year was I wi' him; but waes me! he gaed out with other pretty men in the forty-five – I'll say nae mair about it – My head never settled weel since I lost him; and if I say another word about it, deil a bar will I have the heart to play the night. – Look out, my gentle chap,' he resumed in a different tone, 'ye should see the lights at Brokenburn Glen by this time.'

The Two Drovers

CHAPTER THE FIRST

IT WAS THE day after Doune Fair when my story commences. It had been a brisk market; several dealers had attended from the northern and midland counties in England, and English money had flown so merrily about as to gladden the hearts of the Highland farmers. Many large droves were about to set off for England, under the protection of their owners, or of the topsmen whom they employed in the tedious, laborious, and responsible office of driving the cattle for many hundred miles, from the market where they had been purchased, to the fields or farm-yards where they were to be fattened for the shambles.

The Highlanders, in particular, are masters of this difficult trade of driving, which seems to suit them as well as the trade of war. It affords exercise for all their habits of patient endurance and active exertion. They are required to know perfectly the drove-roads, which lie over the wildest tracts of the country, and to avoid as much as possible the highways, which distress the feet of the bullocks, and the turnpikes, which annoy the spirit of the drover; whereas, on the broad green or grey track, which leads across the pathless moor, the herd not only move at ease and without taxation, but, if they mind their business, may pick up a mouthful of food by the way. At night, the drovers usually sleep along with their cattle, let the weather be what it will; and many of these hardy men do not once rest under a roof during a journey on foot from Lochaber to Lincolnshire. They are paid very highly, for the trust reposed is of the last importance, as it depends on their prudence, vigilance, and honesty, whether the cattle reach the final market in good order, and afford a profit to the grazier. But as they maintain themselves at their own expense, they are especially economical in that particular. At the period we speak of, a Highland drover was victualled for his long and toilsome journey with a few handfuls of oatmeal and two or three onions, renewed from time to time, and a ram's horn filled with whisky, which he used regularly, but sparingly, every night and morning. His dirk, or *skene-dhu* (i.e. black-knife), so worn as to be concealed beneath the arm, or by the folds of the plaid, was his only weapon, excepting the cudgel with which he directed the movements of the cattle. A Highlander was never so happy as on these occasions. There was a variety in the whole

journey, which exercised the Celt's natural curiosity
and love of motion; there were the constant change
of place and scene, the petty adventures incidental
to the traffic, and the intercourse with the various
farmers, graziers, and traders, intermingled with
occasional merry-makings, not the less acceptable
to Donald that they were void of expense; – and
there was the consciousness of superior skill; for
the Highlander, a child amongst flocks, is a prince
amongst herds, and his natural habits induce him to
disdain the shepherd's slothful life, so that he feels
himself nowhere more at home than when following
a gallant drove of his country cattle in the character
of their guardian.

Of the number who left Doune in the morning, and with the purpose we have described, not
a *Glunamie* of them all cocked his bonnet more
briskly, or gartered his tartan hose under knee over a
pair of more promising *spiogs* (legs), than did Robin
Oig M'Combich, called familiarly Robin Oig, that
is, Young, or the Lesser, Robin. Though small of
stature, as the epithet Oig implies, and not very
strongly limbed, he was as light and alert as one
of the deer of his mountains. He had an elasticity
of step, which, in the course of a long march,
made many a stout fellow envy him; and the manner in which he busked his plaid and adjusted his

bonnet, argued a consciousness that so smart a John
Highlandman as himself would not pass unnoticed
among the Lowland lasses. The ruddy cheek, red
lips, and white teeth, set off a countenance, which
had gained by exposure to the weather a healthful
and hardy rather than a rugged hue. If Robin Oig
did not laugh, or even smile frequently, as indeed is
not the practice among his countrymen, his bright
eyes usually gleamed from under his bonnet with
an expression of cheerfulness ready to be turned
into mirth.

The departure of Robin Oig was an incident in the
little town, in and near which he had many friends,
male and female. He was a topping person in his
way, transacted considerable business in his own
behalf, and was intrusted by the best farmers in the
Highlands, in preference to any other drover in that
district. He might have increased his business to any
extent had he condescended to manage it by deputy;
but except a lad or two, sister's sons of his own,
Robin rejected the idea of assistance, conscious,
perhaps, how much his reputation depended upon
his attending in person to the practical discharge of
his duty in every instance. He remained, therefore,
contented with the highest premium given to persons of his description, and comforted himself with
the hopes that few journeys to England might enable

him to conduct a business on his own account, in a manner becoming his birth. For Robin Oig's father, Lachlan M'Combich (or *son of my friend*, his actual clan-surname being M'Gregor), had been so called by the celebrated Rob Roy, because of the particular friendship which had subsisted between the grandsire of Robin and that renowned cateran. Some people even say, that Robin Oig derived his Christian name from one as renowned in the wilds of Lochlomond as ever was his namesake Robin Hood, in the precincts of merry Sherwood. 'Of such ancestry,' as James Boswell says, 'who would not be proud?' Robin Oig was proud accordingly; but his frequent visits to England and to the Lowlands had given him tact enough to know that pretensions, which still gave him a little right to distinction in his own lonely glen, might be both obnoxious and ridiculous if preferred elsewhere. The pride of birth, therefore, was like the miser's treasure, the secret subject of his contemplation, but never exhibited to strangers as a subject of boasting.

Many were the words of gratulation and good-luck which were bestowed on Robin Oig. The judges commended his drove, especially Robin's own property, which were the best of them. Some thrust out their snuff-mulls for the parting pinch – others tendered the *doch-an-dorrach*, or parting cup. All

cried – 'Good-luck travel out with you and come
home with you. – Give you luck in the Saxon
market – brave notes in the *leabhar-dhu*' (black
pocket-book), 'and plenty of English gold in the
sporran' (pouch of goatskin).

The bonny lasses made their adieus more mod-
estly, and more than one, it was said, would have
given her best brooch to be certain that it was upon
her that his eye last rested as he turned towards
the road.

Robin Oig had just given the preliminary '*Hoo-
hoo!*' to urge forward the loiterers of the drove, when
there was a cry behind him.

'Stay, Robin – bide a blink. Here is Janet of
Tomahourich – auld Janet, your father's sister.'

'Plague on her, for an auld Highland witch and
spaewife,' said a farmer from the Carse of Stirling;
'she'll cast some of her cantrips on the cattle.'

'She canna do that,' said another sapient of the
same profession – 'Robin Oig is no the lad to
leave any of them, without tying Saint Mungo's
knot on their tails, and that will put to her speed
the best witch that ever flew over Dimayet upon
a broomstick.'

It may not be indifferent to the reader to know,
that the Highland cattle are peculiarly liable to be
taken, or infected, by spells and witchcraft; which

judicious people guard against, by knitting knots of peculiar complexity on the tuft of hair which terminates the animal's tail.

But the old woman, who was the object of the farmer's suspicion, seemed only busied about the drover, without paying any attention to the drove. Robin, on the contrary, appeared rather impatient of her presence.

'What auld-world fancy,' he said, 'has brought you so early from the ingle-side this morning, Muhme! I am sure I bid you good-even, and had your God-speed, last night.'

'And left me more siller than the useless old woman will use till you come back again, bird of my bosom,' said the sibyl. 'But it is little I would care for the food that nourishes me, or the fire that warms me, or for God's blessed sun itself, if aught but weel should happen to the grandson of my father. So let me walk the *deasil* round you that you may go safe out into the foreign land, and come safe home.'

Robin Oig stopped, half embarrassed, half laughing, and signing to those near that he only complied with the old woman to soothe her humour. In the meantime, she traced around him, with wavering steps, the propitiation, which some have thought has been derived from the Druidical mythology. It consists, as is well known, in the person who makes the *deasil* walking three times round the person who is the object of the ceremony, taking care to move according to the course of the sun. At once, however, she stopped short, and exclaimed, in a voice of alarm and horror, 'Grandson of my father, there is blood on your hand.'

'Hush, for God's sake, aunt,' said Robin Oig; 'you will bring more trouble on yourself with this Taishataragh' (second sight) 'than you will be able to get out of for many a day.'

The old woman only repeated, with a ghastly look, 'There is blood on your hand, and it is English blood. The blood of the Gael is richer and redder. Let us see – let us—'

Ere Robin Oig could prevent her, which, indeed, could only have been done by positive violence, so hasty and peremptory were her proceedings, she had drawn from his side the dirk which lodged in the folds of his plaid, and held it up, exclaiming, although the weapon gleamed clear and bright in the sun, 'Blood, blood – Saxon blood again. Robin Oig M'Combich, go not this day to England!'

'Prutt, trutt,' answered Robin Oig, 'that will never do neither – it would be next thing to running the country. For shame, Muhme – give me the dirk. You cannot tell by the colour the difference betwixt the blood of a black bullock and a white one, and you speak of knowing Saxon from Gaelic blood. All men have their blood from Adam, Muhme. Give me my skene-dhu, and let me go on my road. I should have been half way to Stirling brig by this time. – Give me my dirk and let me go.'

'Never will I give it to you,' said the old woman – 'Never will I quit my hold on your plaid unless you promise me not to wear that unhappy weapon.'

The women around him urged him also, saying few of his aunt's words fell to the ground; and as the Lowland farmers continued to look moodily on the scene, Robin Oig determined to close it at any sacrifice.

'Well, then,' said the young drover, giving the scabbard of the weapon to Hugh Morrison, 'you Lowlanders care nothing for these freats. Keep my dirk for me. I cannot give it you, because it was my father's; but your drove follows ours, and I am content it should be in your keeping, not in mine. – Will this do, Muhme?'

'It must,' said the old woman – 'that is, if the Lowlander is mad enough to carry the knife.'

The strong westlandman laughed aloud.

'Goodwife,' said he, 'I am Hugh Morrison from Glenae, come of the Manly Morrisons of auld lang-syne, that never took short weapon against a man in their lives. And neither needed they: They had their

broadswords, and I have this bit supple,' shewing
a formidable cudgel – 'for dirking ower the board,
I leave that to John Highlandman – Ye needna
snort, none of you Highlanders, and you in especial,
Robin. I'll keep the bit knife, if you are feared for
the auld spaewife's tale, and give it back to you
whenever you want it.'

Robin was not particularly pleased with some part
of Hugh Morrison's speech; but he had learned in
his travels more patience than belonged to his Highland constitution originally, and he accepted the
service of the descendant of the Manly Morrisons,
without finding fault with the rather depreciating
manner in which it was offered.

'If he had not had his morning in his head, and
been but a Dumfries-shire hog into the boot, he
would have spoken more like a gentleman. But
you cannot have more of a sow than a grumph. It's
shame my father's knife should ever slash a haggis
for the like of him.'

Thus saying (but saying it in Gaelic), Robin drove
on his cattle, and waved farewell to all behind him.
He was in the greater haste, because he expected to
join at Falkirk a comrade and brother in profession,
with whom he proposed to travel in company.

Robin Oig's chosen friend was a young Englishman, Harry Wakefield by name, well known at every

northern market, and in his way as much famed and honoured as our Highland driver of bullocks. He was nearly six feet high, gallantly formed to keep the rounds at Smithfield, or maintain the ring at a wrestling match; and although he might have been overmatched, perhaps, among the regular professors of the Fancy, yet, as a yokel or rustic, or a chance customer, he was able to give a bellyful to any amateur of the pugilistic art. Doncaster races saw him in his glory, betting his guinea, and generally successfully; nor was there a main fought in Yorkshire, the feeders being persons of celebrity, at which he was not to be seen, if business permitted. But though a *sprack* lad, and fond of pleasure and its haunts, Harry Wakefield was steady, and not the cautious Robin Oig M'Combich himself was more attentive to the main chance. His holidays were holidays indeed; but his days of work were dedicated to steady and persevering labour. In countenance and temper, Wakefield was the model of Old England's merry yeomen, whose clothyard shafts, in so many hundred battles, asserted her superiority over the nations, and whose good sabres, in our own time, are her cheapest and most assured defence. His mirth was readily excited; for, strong in limb and constitution, and fortunate in circumstances, he was disposed to be pleased with everything about

him; and such difficulties as he might occasionally
encounter, were, to a man of his energy, rather matter of amusement than serious annoyance. With all
the merits of a sanguine temper, our young English
drover was not without his defects. He was irascible,
sometimes to the verge of being quarrelsome; and
perhaps not the less inclined to bring his disputes to
a pugilistic decision, because he found few antagon-
ists able to stand up to him in the boxing ring.

It is difficult to say how Harry Wakefield and
Robin Oig first became intimates; but it is certain a close acquaintance had taken place betwixt
them, although they had apparently few common
subjects of conversation or of interest, so soon as
their talk ceased to be of bullocks. Robin Oig,
indeed spoke the English language rather imper-
fectly upon any other topics but stots and kyloes,
and Harry Wakefield could never bring his broad
Yorkshire tongue to utter a single word of Gaelic.
It was in vain Robin spent a whole morning, during
a walk over Minch Moor in attempting to teach
his companion to utter, with true precision, the
shibboleth *Llhu*, which is the Gaelic for a calf.
From Traquair to Murder-cairn, the hill rung with
the discordant attempts of the Saxon upon the
unmanageable monosyllable, and the heartfelt laugh
which followed every failure. They had, however,

better modes of awakening the echoes; for Wakefield could sing many a ditty to the praise of Moll, Susan, and Cicely, and Robin Oig had a particular gift at whistling interminable pibrochs through all their involutions, and what was more agreeable to his companion's southern ear, knew many of the northern airs, both lively and pathetic, to which Wakefield learned to pipe a bass. Thus, though Robin could hardly have comprehended his companion's stories about horse-racing, and cock-fighting, or fox-hunting, and although his own legends of clan-fights and *creaghs*, varied with talk of Highland goblins and fairy folk, would have been caviare to his companion, they contrived nevertheless to find a degree of pleasure, in each other's company, which had, for three years back induced them to join company and travel together, when the direction of their journey permitted. Each, indeed, found his advantage in this companionship; for where could the Englishman have found a guide through the Western Highlands like Robin Oig M'Combich! and when they were on what Harry called the *right* side of the Border, his patronage, which was extensive, and his purse, which was heavy, were at all times at the service of his Highland friend, and on many occasions his liberality did him genuine yeoman's service.

CHAPTER THE SECOND

Were ever two such loving friends!—
   How could they disagree?
O thus it was, he loved him dear,
   And thought how to requite him,
And having no friend left but he,
   He did resolve to fight him.

DUKE UPON DUKE

THE PAIR OF friends had traversed with their usual cordiality the grassy wilds of Liddesdale, and crossed the opposite part of Cumberland, emphatically called The Waste. In these solitary regions, the cattle under the charge of our drovers derived their subsistence chiefly by picking their food as they went along the drove-road, or sometimes by the tempting opportunity of a *start and owerloup*, or invasion of the neighbouring pasture, where an occasion presented itself. But now the scene changed before them; they were descending towards a fertile and enclosed country, where no such liberties could be taken with impunity, or without a previous arrangement and bargain with the possessors of the ground. This was more especially the case, as a great northern fair was upon the eve of taking place, where both the Scotch and English drover expected to dispose of a part of their cattle, which it was desirable to produce in the market, rested and in good order. Fields were therefore difficult to be obtained, and only upon high terms. This necessity occasioned a temporary separation betwixt the two friends, who went to bargain, each as he could, for the separate accommodation of his herd. Unhappily it chanced that both of them, unknown to each other, thought of bargaining for the ground they wanted on the property of a country gentleman of some fortune, whose estate lay in the neighbourhood. The English drover applied to the bailiff on the property, who was known to him. It chanced that the Cumbrian Squire, who had entertained some suspicions of his manager's honesty, was taking occasional measures to ascertain how far they were well founded, and had desired that any inquiries about his enclosures, with a view to occupy them for a temporary purpose, should be referred to himself. As, however, Mr Ireby had gone the day before upon a journey of some miles' distance to the northward, the bailiff chose to consider the check upon his full powers as for the time removed, and concluded that he should best consult his master's interest, and perhaps his own, in making an agreement with Harry Wakefield. Meanwhile, ignorant of what his comrade was doing, Robin Oig, on his side, chanced to be overtaken by a good-looking smart little man upon a pony, most knowingly hogged and cropped, as was then the fashion, the rider wearing tight leather breeches, and long-necked bright spurs. This cavalier asked one or two pertinent questions about markets and the price of stock. So Robin seeing him a well-judging civil gentleman, took the freedom to ask him whether he could let him know if there was any grass-land to be let in that neighbourhood, for the temporary accommodation of his drove. He could not have put the question to more willing ears. The gentleman of the buckskin was the proprietor, with whose bailiff Harry Wakefield had dealt, or was in the act of dealing.

'Thou art in good luck, my canny Scot,' said Mr Ireby, 'to have spoken to me, for I see thy cattle have done their day's work, and I have at my disposal the only field within three miles that is to be let in these parts.'

'The drove can pe gang two, three, four miles very pratty weel indeed' – said the cautious Highlander;

'put what would his honour be axing for the peasts pe the head, if she was to tak the park for twa or three days?'

'We won't differ, Sawney, if you let me have six stots for winterers, in the way of reason.'

'And which peasts wad your honour pe for having?'

'Why – let me see – the two black – the dun one – yon doddy – him with the twisted horn – the brockit – How much by the head?'

'Ah,' said Robin, 'your honour is a shudge – a real shudge – I couldna have set off the pest six peasts petter mysell, me that ken them as if they were my pairns, puir things.'

'Well, how much per head, Sawney?' continued Mr Ireby.

'It was high markets at Doune and Falkirk,' answered Robin.

And thus the conversation proceeded, until they had agreed on the *prix juste* for the bullocks, the Squire throwing in the temporary accommodation of the enclosure for the cattle into the boot, and Robin making, as he thought, a very good bargain, provided the grass was but tolerable. The squire walked his pony alongside of the drove, partly to shew him the way, and see him put into possession of the field, and partly to learn the latest news of the northern markets.

They arrived at the field, and the pasture seemed excellent. But what was their surprise when they saw the bailiff quietly inducting the cattle of Harry Wakefield into the grassy Goshen which had just been assigned to those of Robin Oig M'Combich by the proprietor himself! Squire Ireby set spurs to his horse, dashed up to his servant, and learning what had passed between the parties, briefly informed the English drover that his bailiff had let the ground without his authority, and that he might seek grass for his cattle wherever he would, since he was to get none there. At the same time he rebuked his servant severely for having transgressed his commands, and ordered him instantly to assist in ejecting the hungry and weary cattle of Harry Wakefield, which were just beginning to enjoy a meal of unusual plenty, and to introduce those of his comrade, whom the English drover now began to consider as a rival.

The feelings which arose in Wakefield's mind would have induced him to resist Mr Ireby's decision; but every Englishman has a tolerable accurate sense of law and justice, and John Fleecebumpkin, the bailiff, having acknowledged that he had exceeded his commission, Wakefield saw nothing else for it than to collect his hungry and disappointed charge, and drive them on to seek quarters elsewhere. Robin Oig saw what had happened with regret, and hastened to offer to his English friend to share with him the disputed possession. But Wakefield's pride was severely hurt and he answered disdainfully, 'Take it all, man – take it all – never make two bites of a cherry – thou canst talk over the gentry, and blear a plain man's eye – Out upon you, man – I would not kiss any man's dirty latchets for leave to bake in his oven.'

Robin Oig, sorry but not surprised at his comrade's displeasure, hastened to entreat his friend to wait but an hour till he had gone to the Squire's house to receive payment for the cattle he had sold, and he would come back and help him to drive the cattle into some convenient place of rest, and explain to him the whole mistake they had both of them fallen into. But the Englishman continued indignant: 'Thou hast been selling, hast thou? Ay, ay – thou is a cunning lad for kenning the hours of bargaining. Go to the devil with thyself, for I will ne'er see thy fause loon's visage again – thou should be ashamed to look me in the face.'

'I am ashamed to look no man in the face,' said Robin Oig, something moved; 'and, moreover, I will look you in the face this blessed day, if you will bide at the Clachan down yonder.'

'Mayhap you had as well keep away,' said his

comrade; and turning his back on his former friend, he collected his unwilling associates, assisted by the bailiff, who took some real and some affected interest in seeing Wakefield accommodated.

After spending some time in negotiating with more than one of the neighbouring farmers, who could not, or would not, afford the accommodation desired, Henry Wakefield at last, and in his necessity, accomplished his point by means of the landlord of the alehouse at which Robin Oig and he had agreed to pass the night, when they first separated from each other. Mine host was content to let him turn his cattle on a piece of barren moor, at a price little less than the bailiff had asked for the disputed enclosure; and the wretchedness of the pasture, as well as the price paid for it, were set down as exaggerations of the breach of faith and friendship of his Scottish crony. This turn of Wakefield's passions was encouraged by the bailiff (who had his own reasons for being offended against poor Robin, as having been the unwitting cause of his falling into disgrace with his master), as well as by the innkeeper, and two or three chance guests, who stimulated the drover in his resentment against his quondam associate, – some from the ancient grudge against the Scots, which, when it exists anywhere, is to be found lurking in the border counties, and some from the general love of mischief, which characterises mankind in all ranks of life, to the honour of Adam's children be it spoken. Good John Barleycorn also, who always heightens and exaggerates the prevailing passions, be they angry or kindly, was not wanting in his offices on this occasion; and confusion to false friends and hard masters, was pledged in more than one tankard.

In the meanwhile Mr Ireby found some amusement in detaining the northern drover at his ancient hall. He caused a cold round of beef to be placed before the Scot in the butler's pantry, together with a foaming tankard of home-brewed, and took pleasure in seeing the hearty appetite with which these unwonted edibles were discussed by Robin Oig M'Combich. The Squire himself lighting his pipe, compounded between his patrician dignity and his love of agricultural gossip, by walking up and down while he conversed with his guest.

'I passed another drove,' said the Squire 'with one of your countrymen behind them – they were something less beasts than your drove, doddies most of them – a big man was with them – none of your kilts though, but a decent pair of breeches – D'ye know who he may be?'

'Hout aye – that might, could, and would be Hughie Morrison – I didna think he could hae peen sae weel up. He has made a day on us; but his Argyleshires will have wearied shanks. How far was he pehind?'

'I think about six or seven miles,' answered the Squire, 'for I passed them at the Christenbury Crag, and I overtook you at the Hollan Bush. If his beasts be leg-weary, he will be maybe selling bargains.'

'Na, na, Hughie Morrison is no the man for pargains – ye maun come to some Highland body like Robin Oig hersell for the like of these – put I maun pe wishing you goot night, and twenty of them let alane ane, and I maun down to the Clachan to see if the lad Harry Waakfelt is out of his humdudgeons yet.'

The party at the alehouse were still in full talk, and the treachery of Robin Oig still the theme of conversation, when the supposed culprit entered the apartment. His arrival, as usually happens in such a case, put an instant stop to the discussion of which he had furnished the subject, and he was received by the company assembled with that chilling silence, which, more than a thousand exclamations, tells an intruder that he is unwelcome. Surprised and offended, but not appalled by the reception which he experienced, Robin entered with an undaunted and even a haughty air, attempted no greeting, as he saw he was received with none, and placed himself by the side of the fire, a little apart from a table, at which Harry Wakefield, the bailiff, and two or three other persons, were seated. The ample Cumbrian kitchen would have afforded plenty of room, even for a larger separation.

Robin thus seated, proceeded to light his pipe and call for a pint of twopenny.

'We have no twopence ale,' answered Ralph Heskett the landlord; 'but as thou find'st thy own tobacco, it's like thou mayst find thy own liquor too – it's the wont of thy country, I wot.'

'Shame, goodman,' said the landlady, a blithe bustling housewife, hastening herself to supply the guest with liquor – 'thou knowest well enow what the strange man wants, and it's thy trade to be civil, man. Thou shouldst know, that if the Scot likes a small pot, he pays a sure penny.'

Without taking any notice of this nuptial dialogue, the Highlander took the flagon in his hand, and addressing the company generally, drank the interesting toast of 'Good markets,' to the party assembled.

'The better that the wind blew fewer dealers from the north,' said one of the farmers, 'and fewer Highland runts to eat up the English meadows.'

'Saul of my pody, put you are wrang there, my friend,' answered Robin, with composure; 'it is your fat Englishmen that eat up our Scots cattle, puir things.'

'I wish there was a summat to eat up their drovers,' said another; 'a plain Englishman canna make bread within a kenning of them.'

'Or an honest servant keep his master's favour, but they will come sliding in between him and the sunshine,' said the bailiff.

'If these pe jokes,' said Robin Oig, with the same composure, 'there is ower mony jokes upon one man.'

'It is no joke, but downright earnest,' said the bailiff. 'Harkye, Mr Robin Ogg, or whatever is your name, it's right we should tell you that we are all of one opinion, and that is, that you, Mr Robin Ogg, have behaved to our friend, Mr Harry Wakefield here, like a raff and a blackguard.'

'Nae doubt, nae doubt,' answered Robin, with great composure; 'and you are a set of very pretty judges, for whose prains or pehaviour I wad not gie a pinch of sneeshing. If Mr Harry Waakfelt kens where he is wranged, he kens where he may be righted.'

'He speaks truth,' said Wakefield, who had listened to what passed, divided between the offence which he had taken at Robin's late behaviour, and the revival of his habitual feelings of regard.

He now rose, and went towards Robin, who got up from his seat as he approached, and held out his hand.

'That's right, Harry – go it – serve him out,' resounded an all sides – 'tip him the nailer – shew him the mill.'

'Hold your peace all of you, and be—,' said Wakefield; and then addressing his comrade, he took him by the extended hand, with something alike of respect and defiance. 'Robin,' he said, 'thou hast used me ill enough this day; but if you mean, like a frank fellow, to shake hands, and take a tussle for love on the sod, why I'll forgie thee man, and we shall be better friends than ever.'

'And would it not pe petter to pe cood friends without more of the matter?' said Robin; 'we will pe much better friendships with our panes hale than proken.'

Harry Wakefield dropped the hand of his friend, or rather threw it from him.

'I did not think I had been keeping company for three years with a coward.'

'Coward pelongs to none of my name,' said Robin, whose eyes began to kindle, but keeping the command of his temper. 'It was no coward's legs or hands, Harry Waskfelt, that drew you out of the fords of Frew, when you was drifting ower the plack rock, and every eel in the river expected his share of you.'

'And that is true enough, too,' said the Englishman, struck by the appeal.

'Adzooks!' exclaimed the bailiff – 'sure Harry Wakefield, the nattiest lad at Whitson Tryste, Wooler Fair, Carlisle Sands, or Stagshaw Bank, is not going to show white feather? Ah, this comes of living so long with kilts and bonnets – men forget the use of their daddles.'

'I may teach you, Master Fleecebumpkin, that I have not lost the use of mine,' said Wakefield, and then went on. 'This will never do, Robin. We must have a turn-up, or we shall be the talk of the country side. I'll be d—d if I hurt thee – I'll put on the gloves gin thou like. Come, stand forward like a man.'

'To pe peaten like a dog,' said Robin; 'is there any reason in that? If you think I have done you wrong, I'll go before your shudge, though I neither know his law nor his language.'

A general cry of 'No, no – no law, no lawyer! a bellyful and be friends,' was echoed by the bystanders.

'But,' continued Robin, 'if I am to fight, I have

no skill to fight like a jackanapes, with hands and nails.'

'How would you fight then!' said his antagonist; 'though I am thinking it would be hard to bring you to the scratch anyhow.'

'I would fight with proadswords, and sink point on the first plood drawn – like a gentleman's.'

A loud shout of laughter followed the proposal, which indeed had rather escaped from poor Robin's swelling heart, than been the dictate of his sober judgment.

'Gentleman, quotha!' was echoed on all sides, with a shout of unextinguishable laughter; 'a very pretty gentleman, God wot – Canst get two swords for the gentlemen to fight with, Ralph Heskett?'

'No, but I can send to the armoury at Carlisle, and lend them two forks, to be making shift with in the meantime.'

'Tush, man,' said another, 'the bonny Scots come into the world with the blue bonnet on their heads, and dirk and pistol at their belt.'

'Best send post,' said Mr Fleecebumpkin, 'to the Squire of Corby Castle, to come and stand second to the *gentleman*.'

In the midst of this torrent of general ridicule the Highlander instinctively griped beneath the folds of his plaid.

'But it's better not,' he said in his own language. 'A hundred curses on the swine-eaters, who know neither decency nor civility!'

'Make room, the pack of you,' he said, advancing to the door.

But his former friend interposed his sturdy bulk, and opposed his leaving the house; and when Robin Oig attempted to make his way by force, he hit him down on the floor, with as much ease as a boy bowls down a nine-pin.

'A ring, a ring!' was now shouted, until the dark rafters, and the hams that hung on them, trembled again, and the very platters on the *bink* clattered against each other. 'Well done, Harry' – 'Give it him home, Harry' – 'Take care of him now – he sees his own blood!'

Such were the exclamations, while the High-lander, starting from the ground, all his coldness and caution lost in frantic rage, sprung at his antagonist with the fury, the activity, and the vindictive purpose, of an incensed tiger-cat. But when could rage encounter science and temper! Robin Oig again went down in the unequal contest; and as the blow was necessarily a severe one, he lay motionless on the floor of the kitchen. The landlady ran to offer some aid, but Mr Fleecebumpkin would not permit her to approach.

'Let him alone,' he said, 'he will come to within time, and come up to the scratch again. He has not got half his broth yet.'

'He has got all I mean to give him, though,' said his antagonist, whose heart began to relent towards his old associate; 'and I would rather by half give the rest to yourself, Mr Fleecebumpkin, for you pretend to know a thing or two, and Robin had not art enough even to peel before setting to, but fought with his plaid dangling about him. – Stand up, Robin, my man! all friends now; and let me hear the man that will speak a word against you, or your country, for your sake.'

Robin Oig was still under the dominion of his passion, and eager to renew the onset; but being withheld on the one side by the peace-making Dame Heskett, and on the other, aware that Wakefield no longer meant to renew the combat, his fury sunk into gloomy sullenness.

'Come, come, never grudge so much at it, man,' said the brave-spirited Englishman, with the placability of his country, 'shake hands, and we will be better friends than ever.'

'Friends!' exclaimed Robin Oig, with strong emphasis – 'friends! – Never. Look to yourself, Harry Waakfelt.'

'Then the curse of Cromwell on your proud Scots

stomach, as the man says in the play, and you may do your worst, and be d—d; for one man can say nothing more to another after a tussle, than that he is sorry for it.'

On these terms the friends parted; Robin Oig drew out, in silence, a piece of money, threw it on the table, and then left the alehouse. But turning at the door, he shook his hand at Wakefield, pointing with his forefinger upwards, in a manner which might imply either a threat or a caution. He then disappeared in the moonlight.

Some words passed after his departure, between the bailiff, who piqued himself on being a little of a bully, and Harry Wakefield, who, with generous inconsistency, was now not indisposed to begin a new combat in defence of Robin Oig's reputation, 'although he could not use his daddles like an Englishman, as it did not come natural to him.' But Dame Heskett prevented this second quarrel from coming to a head by her peremptory interference. 'There should be no more fighting in her house,' she said; 'there had been too much already. – And you, Mr Wakefield, may live to learn,' she added, 'what it is to make a deadly enemy out of a good friend.'

'Pshaw, dame! Robin Oig is an honest fellow, and will never keep malice.'

'Do not trust to that – you do not know the dour temper of the Scots, though you have dealt with them so often. I have a right to know them, my mother being a Scot.'

'And so is well seen on her daughter,' said Ralph Heskett.

This nuptial sarcasm gave the discourse another turn; fresh customers entered the tap-room or kitchen, and others left it. The conversation turned on the expected markets, and the report of prices from different parts both of Scotland and England – treaties were commenced, and Harry Wakefield was lucky enough to find a chap for a part of his drove, and at a very considerable profit; an event of consequence more than sufficient to blot out all remembrances of the unpleasant scuffle in the earlier part of the day. But there remained one party from whose mind that recollection could not have been wiped away by the possession of every head of cattle betwixt Esk and Eden.

This was Robin Oig M'Combich. – 'That I should have had no weapon,' he said, 'and for the first time in my life! – Blighted be the tongue that bids the Highlander part with the dirk – the dirk – ha! the English blood! – My Muhme's word – when did her word fall to the ground?'

The recollection of the fatal prophecy confirmed

the deadly intention which instantly sprung up in his mind.

'Ha! Morrison cannot be many miles behind; and if it were a hundred, what then?'

His impetuous spirit had now a fixed purpose and motive of action, and he turned the light foot of his country towards the wilds, through which he knew, by Mr Ireby's report, that Morrison was advancing. His mind was wholly engrossed by the sense of injury – injury sustained from a friend; and by the desire of vengeance on one whom he now accounted his most bitter enemy. The treasured ideas of self-importance and self-opinion – of ideal birth and quality, had become more precious to him (like the hoard to the miser), because he could only enjoy them in secret. But that hoard was pillaged; the idols which he had secretly worshipped had been desecrated and profaned. Insulted, abused, and beaten, he was no longer worthy, in his own opinion, of the name he bore, or the lineage which he belonged to – nothing was left to him – nothing but revenge; and, as the reflection added a galling spur to every step, he determined it should be as sudden and signal as the offence.'

When Robin Oig left the door of the alehouse, seven or eight English miles at least lay betwixt Morrison and him. The advance of the former was slow, limited by the sluggish pace of his cattle; the last left behind him stubble-field and hedge-row, crag and dark heath, all glittering with frost-rime in the broad November moonlight, at the rate of six miles an hour. And now the distant lowing of Morrison's cattle is heard; and now they are seen creeping like moles in size and slowness of motion on the broad face of the moor; and now he meets them – passes them, and stops their conductor.

'May good betide us,' said the Southlander – 'Is this you, Robin M'Combich, or your wraith?'

'It is Robin Oig M'Combich,' answered the Highlander, 'and it is not. – But never mind that, put pe giving me the skene-dhu.'

'What! you are for back to the Highlands – The devil! – Have you selt all off before the fair? This beats all for quick markets!'

'I have not sold – I am not going north – May pe I will never go north again. – Give me pack my dirk, Hugh Morrison, or there will pe words petween us.'

'Indeed, Robin, I'll be better advised before I gie it back to you – it is a wanchancy weapon in a Highlandman's hand, and I am thinking you will be about some barns-breaking.'

'Prutt, trutt! let me have my weapon,' said Robin Oig, impatiently.

'Hooly and fairly,' said his well-meaning friend. 'I'll tell you what will do better than these dirking doings – Ye ken Highlander, and Lowlander, and Border-men, are a' ae man's bairns when you are over the Scot's dyke. See, the Eskdale callants, and fighting Charlie of Liddesdale, and the Lockerby lads, and the four Dandies of Lustruther, and a wheen mair gray plaids, are coming up behind; and if you are wranged, there is the hand of a Manly Morrison, we'll see you righted, if Carlisle and Stanwix baith took up the feud.'

'To tell you the truth,' said Robin Oig, desirous of eluding the suspicions of his friend, 'I have enlisted with a party of the Black Watch, and must march off tomorrow morning.'

'Enlisted! Were you mad or drunk? – You must buy yourself off – I can lend you twenty notes, and twenty to that, if the drove sell.'

'I thank you – thank ye, Hughie; but I go with good will the gate that I am going, – so the dirk – the dirk!'

'There it is for you then, since less wunna serve. But think on what I was saying. – Waes me, it will be sair news in the braes of Balquidder, that Robin Oig M'Combich should have run an ill gate and ta'en on.'

'Ill news in Balquidder, indeed!' echoed poor

Robin: 'but Cot speed you, Hughie, and send you good marcats. Ye winna meet with Robin Oig again, either at tryste or fair.'

So saying, he shook hastily the hand of his acquaintance, and set out in the direction from which he had advanced, with the spirit of his former pace.

'There is something wrang with the lad,' muttered the Morrison to himself; 'but we will maybe see better into it the morn's morning.'

But long ere the morning dawned, the catastrophe of our tale had taken place. It was two hours after the affray had happened, and it was totally forgotten by almost every one, when Robin Oig returned to Heskett's inn. The place was filled at once by various sorts of men, and with noises corresponding to their character. There were the grave low sounds of men engaged in busy traffic, with the laugh, the song, and the riotous jest of those who had nothing to do but to enjoy themselves. Among the last was Harry Wakefield, who, amidst a grinning group of smock-frocks, hobnailed shoes, and jolly English physiognomies, was trolling forth the old ditty,

> What though my name be Roger,
> Who drives the plough and cart—

when he was interrupted by a well-known voice saying in a high and stern tone, marked by the sharp Highland accent, 'Harry Waakfelt – if you be a man stand up!'

'What is the matter? – what is it?' the guests demanded of each other.

'It is only a d—d Scotsman,' said Fleecebumpkin, who was by this time very drunk, 'whom Harry Wakefield helped to his broth today, who is now come to have *his cauld kail* het again.'

'Harry Waakfelt,' repeated the same ominous summons, 'stand up, if you be a man!'

There is something in the tone of deep and concentrated passion, which attracts attention and imposes awe, even by the very sound. The guests shrunk back on every side, and gazed at the Highlander as he stood in the middle of them, his brows bent, and his features rigid with resolution.

'I will stand up with all my heart, Robin, my boy, but it shall be to shake hands with you, and drink down all unkindness. It is not the fault of your heart, man, that you don't know how to clench your hands.'

By this time he stood opposite to his antagonist; his open and unsuspecting look strangely contrasted with the stern purpose, which gleamed wild, dark, and vindictive in the eyes of the Highlander.

''Tis not thy fault, man, that, not having the luck to be an Englishman, thou canst not fight more than a school-girl.'

'I *can* fight,' answered Robin Oig sternly, but calmly, 'and you shall know it. You, Harry Waakfelt, shewed me today how the Saxon churls fight – I shew you now how the Highland Dunnie-wassal fights.'

He seconded the word with the action, and plunged the dagger, which he suddenly displayed, into the broad breast of the English yeoman, with such fatal certainty and force, that the hilt made a hollow sound against the breast-bone, and the double-edged point split the very heart of his victim. Harry Wakefield fell and expired with a single groan. His assassin next seized the bailiff by the collar, and offered the bloody poniard to his throat, whilst dread and surprise rendered the man incapable of defence.

'It were very just to lay you beside him,' he said, 'but the blood of a base pick-thank shall never mix on my father's dirk, with that of a brave man.'

As he spoke, he cast the man from him with so much force that he fell on the floor, while Robin, with his other hand, threw the fatal weapon into the blazing turf-fire.

'There,' he said, 'take me who likes – and let fire cleanse blood if it can.'

The pause of astonishment still continuing, Robin Oig asked for a peace-officer, and a constable having stepped out, he surrendered himself to his custody.

'A bloody night's work you have made of it,' said the constable.

'Your own fault,' said the Highlander. 'Had you kept his hands off me twa hours since, he would have been now as well and merry as he was twa minutes since.'

'It must be sorely answered,' said the peace-officer.

'Never you mind that – death pays all debts; it will pay that too.'

The horror of the bystanders began now to give way to indignation; and the sight of a favourite companion murdered in the midst of them, the provocation being, in their opinion, so utterly inadequate to the excess of vengeance, might have induced them to kill the perpetrator of the deed even upon the very spot. The constable, however, did his duty on this occasion, and with the assistance of some of the more reasonable persons present, procured horses to guard the prisoner to Carlisle, to abide his doom at the next assizes. While the escort was preparing, the prisoner neither expressed the least interest, nor attempted the slightest reply. Only, before he was carried from the fatal apartment, he desired to look at the dead body, which, raised from the floor, had been deposited upon the large table (at the head of which Harry Wakefield had presided but a few minutes before, full of life, vigour, and animation), until the surgeons should examine the mortal wound. The face of the corpse was decently covered with a napkin. To the surprise and horror of the bystanders, which displayed itself in a general *Ah!* drawn through clenched teeth and half-shut lips, Robin Oig removed the cloth, and gazed with a mournful but steady eye on the lifeless visage, which had been so lately animated, that the smile of good-humoured confidence in his own strength, of conciliation at once, and contempt towards his enemy, still curled his lip. While those present expected that the wound, which had so lately flooded the apartment with gore, would send forth fresh streams at the touch of the homicide, Robin Oig replaced the covering, with the brief exclamation – 'He was a pretty man!'

My story is nearly ended. The unfortunate Highlander stood his trial at Carlisle. I was myself present, and as a young Scottish lawyer, or barrister at least, and reputed a man of some quality, the politeness of the Sheriff of Cumberland offered me a place on the bench. The facts of the case were proved in the manner I have related them; and whatever might be at first the prejudice of the audience against a crime so un-English as that of assassination from revenge, yet when the rooted national prejudices of the prisoner had been explained, which made him consider himself as stained with indelible dishonour, when subjected to personal violence; when his previous patience, moderation, and endurance, were considered, the generosity of the English audience was inclined to regard his crime as the wayward aberration of a false idea of honour rather than as flowing from a heart naturally savage, or perverted by habitual vice. I shall never forget the charge of the venerable Judge to the jury, although not at that time liable to be much affected either by that which was eloquent or pathetic.

'We have had,' he said, 'in the previous part of our duty' (alluding to some former trials), 'to discuss crimes which infer disgust and abhorrence, while they call down the well-merited vengeance of the law. It is now our still more melancholy task to apply its salutary though severe enactments to a case of a very singular character in which the crime (for a crime it is, and a deep one) arose less out of the malevolence of the heart, than the error of the understanding – less from any idea of committing

wrong, than from an unhappily perverted notion of
that which is right. Here we have two men, highly
esteemed, it has been stated, in their rank of life,
and attached, it seems, to each other as friends,
one of whose lives has been already sacrificed to
a punctilio, and the other is about to prove the
vengeance of the offended laws; and yet both may
claim our commiseration at least, as men acting in
ignorance of each other's national prejudices, and
unhappily misguided rather than voluntarily erring
from the path of right conduct.

'In the original cause of the misunderstanding,
we must in justice give the right to the prisoner at
the bar. He had acquired possession of the enclosure, which was the object of competition, by a
legal contract with the proprietor, Mr Ireby; and
yet, when accosted with reproaches undeserved in
themselves, and galling doubtless to a temper at
least sufficiently susceptible of passion, he offered
notwithstanding to yield up half his acquisition, for
the sake of peace and good neighbourhood, and his
amicable proposal was rejected with scorn. Then
follows the scene at Mr Heskett the publican's, and
you will observe how the stranger was treated by
the deceased, and, I am sorry to observe, by those
around, who seem to have urged him in a manner
which was aggravating in the highest degree. While

he asked for peace and for composition, and offered submission to a magistrate, or to a mutual arbiter, the prisoner was insulted by a whole company, who seem on this occasion to have forgotten the national maxim of 'fair play;' and while attempting to escape from the place in peace, he was intercepted, struck down, and beaten to the effusion of his blood.

'Gentlemen of the Jury, it was with some impatience that I heard my learned brother, who opened the case for the crown, give an unfavourable turn to the prisoner's conduct on this occasion. He said the prisoner was afraid to encounter his antagonist in fair fight, or to submit to the laws of the ring; and that therefore, like a cowardly Italian, he had recourse to his fatal stiletto, to murder the man whom he dared not meet in manly encounter. I observed the prisoner shrink from this part of the accusation with the abhorrence natural to a brave man; and as I would wish to make my words impressive, when I point his real crime, I must secure his opinion of my impartiality, by rebutting everything that seems to me a false accusation. There can be no doubt that the prisoner is a man of resolution – too much resolution – I wish to Heaven that he had less, or rather that he had had a better education to regulate it.

'Gentlemen, as to the laws my brother talks of,

they may be known in the Bull-ring or the Bear-
garden, or the Cockpit, but they are not known here.
Or, if they should be so far admitted as furnishing
a species of proof that no malice was intended in
this sort of combat, from which fatal accidents do
sometimes arise, it can only be so admitted when
both parties are in *pari casu*, equally acquainted
with, and equally willing to refer themselves to,
that species of arbitrement. But will it be contended
that a man of superior rank and education is to
be subjected, or is obliged to subject himself, to
this coarse and brutal strife, perhaps in opposition
to a younger, stronger, or more skilful opponent?
Certainly even the pugilistic code, if founded upon
the fair play of Merry Old England, as my brother
alleges it to be, can contain nothing so preposterous. And, gentlemen of the jury, if the laws would
support an English gentleman, wearing, we will
suppose, his sword, in defending himself by force
against a violent personal aggression of the nature
offered to this prisoner, they will not less protect
a foreigner and a stranger, involved in the same
unpleasing circumstances. If, therefore, gentlemen
of the jury when thus pressed by a *vis major*, the
object of obloquy to a whole company, and of
direct violence from one at least, and, as he might
reasonably apprehend, from more, the panel had

produced the weapon which his countrymen, as we are informed, generally carry about their persons, and the same unhappy circumstance had ensued which you have heard detailed in evidence, I could not in my conscience have asked from you a verdict of murder. The prisoner's personal defence might indeed, even in that case, have gone more or less beyond the *Moderamen inculpatæ tutelæ*, spoken of by lawyers, but the punishment incurred would have been that of manslaughter, not of murder. I beg leave to add, that I should have thought this milder species of charge was demanded in the case supposed, notwithstanding the statute of James I. cap. 8, which takes the case of slaughter by stabbing with a short weapon, even without malice prepense, out of the benefit of clergy. For this statute of stabbing, as it is termed, arose out of a temporary cause; and as the real guilt is the same, whether the slaughter be committed by the dagger, or by sword or pistol, the benignity of the modern law places them all on the same, or nearly the same footing.

'But, gentlemen of the jury, the pinch of the case lies in the interval of two hours interposed betwixt the reception of the injury and the fatal retaliation. In the heat of affray and *chaude mêlée*, law, compassionating the infirmities of humanity, makes allowance for the passions which rule such a stormy moment – for the sense of present pain, for the apprehension of further injury, for the difficulty of ascertaining with due accuracy the precise degree of violence which is necessary to protect the person of the individual, without annoying or injuring the assailant more than is absolutely requisite. But the time necessary to walk twelve miles, however speedily performed, was an interval sufficient for the prisoner to have recollected himself; and the violence with which he carried his purpose into effect, with so many circumstances of deliberate determination, could neither be induced by the passion of anger, nor that of fear. It was the purpose and the act of predetermined revenge, for which law neither can, will, nor ought to have sympathy or allowance.

'It is true, we may repeat to ourselves, in alleviation of this poor man's unhappy action, that his case is a very peculiar one. The country which he inhabits was, in the days of many now alive, inaccessible to the laws, not only of England, which have not even yet penetrated thither, but to those to which our neighbours of Scotland are subjected, and which must be supposed to be, and no doubt actually are, founded upon the general principles of justice and equity which pervade every civilised country. Amongst their mountains, as among the

North American Indians, the various tribes were wont to make war upon each other, so that each man was obliged to go armed for his own protection. These men, from the ideas which they entertained of their own descent and of their own consequence, regarded themselves as so many cavaliers or men-at-arms, rather than as the peasantry of a peaceful country. Those laws of the ring, as my brother terms them, were unknown to the race of warlike mountaineers; that decision of quarrels by no other weapons than those which nature has given every man, must to them have seemed as vulgar and as preposterous as to the Noblesse of France. Revenge, on the other hand, must have been as familiar to their habits of society as to those of the Cherokees or Mohawks. It is, indeed, as described by Bacon, at bottom a kind of wild untutored justice; for the fear of retaliation must withhold the hands of the oppressor where there is no regular law to check daring violence. But though all this may be granted, and though we may allow that, such having been the case of the Highlands in the days of the prisoner's fathers, many of the opinions and sentiments must still continue to influence the present generation, it cannot, and ought not, even in this most painful case, to alter the administration of the law, either in your hands, gentlemen of the jury, or in mine.

The first object of civilisation is to place the general
protection of the law, equally administered, in the
room of that wild justice, which every man cut and
carved for himself, according to the length of his
sword and the strength of his arm. The law says to
the subjects, with a voice only inferior to that of the
Deity, "Vengeance is mine." The instant that there
is time for passion to cool, and reason to interpose,
an injured party must become aware, that the law
assumes the exclusive cognizance of the right and
wrong betwixt the parties, and opposes her invio-
lable buckler to every attempt of the private party
to right himself. I repeat, that this unhappy man
ought personally to be the object rather of our pity
than our abhorrence, for he failed in his ignorance,
and from mistaken notions of honour. But his crime
is not the less that of murder, gentlemen, and, in
your high and important office, it is your duty so to
find. Englishmen have their angry passions as well as
Scots; and should this man's action remain unpun-
ished, you may unsheath, under various pretences,
a thousand daggers betwixt the Land's-end and the
Orkneys.'

   The venerable Judge thus ended what, to judge by
his apparent emotion, and by the tears which filled
his eyes, was really a painful task. The jury, according to his instructions, brought in a verdict of Guilty;

and Robin Oig M'Combich, *alias* M'Gregor, was sentenced to death, and left for execution, which took place accordingly. He met his fate with great firmness, and acknowledged the justice of his sentence. But he repelled indignantly the observations of those who accused him of attacking an unarmed man. 'I give a life for the life I took,' he said, 'and what can I do more?'